Mama,
I Can't Sleep

Written by Brigitte Raab

Illustrated by Manuela Olten

Translated by Connie Stradling Morby

Sky Pony Press
New York

Mama, I can't sleep. I just can't. I close my eyes very tight for a long time. But then they open again, and I'm still awake.

Try again. Your bed is so comfortable. Snuggle up in your blanket with your little leopard and close your eyes. All creatures sleep. Even the real leopards in Africa.

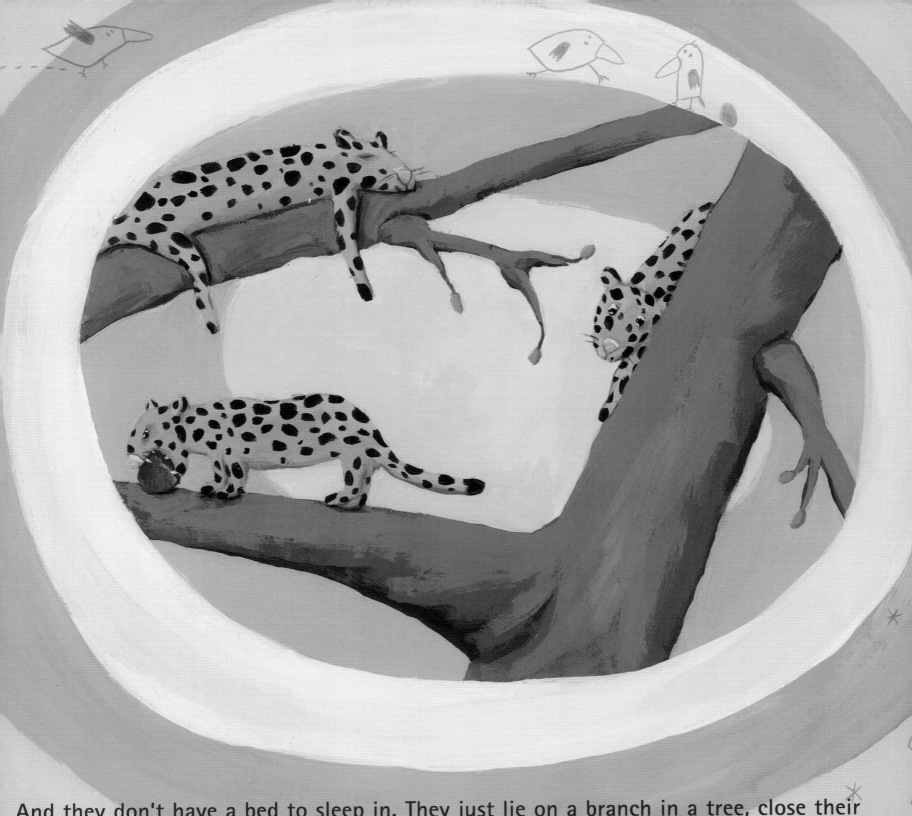

And they don't have a bed to sleep in. They just lie on a branch in a tree, close their eyes, and sleep. Without a blanket, without a pillow, and without falling down.

Mama, I can't sleep.

Even though I tried it like the leopards in Africa. But here in the tree, it's not comfortable at all. I'm freezing, and I have to be careful so that I don't fall down. That's why I can't close my eyes. And my little leopard has already fallen down twice.

You're not a leopard either.
Every creature sleeps differently.
Storks like to sleep standing on one leg.
The other leg they tuck in their feathers.
From time to time they change legs.

Mama, I can't sleep.

Even though I stood on one leg like a s

But I have to balance a lot so I won't tip

Now I'm wide awa

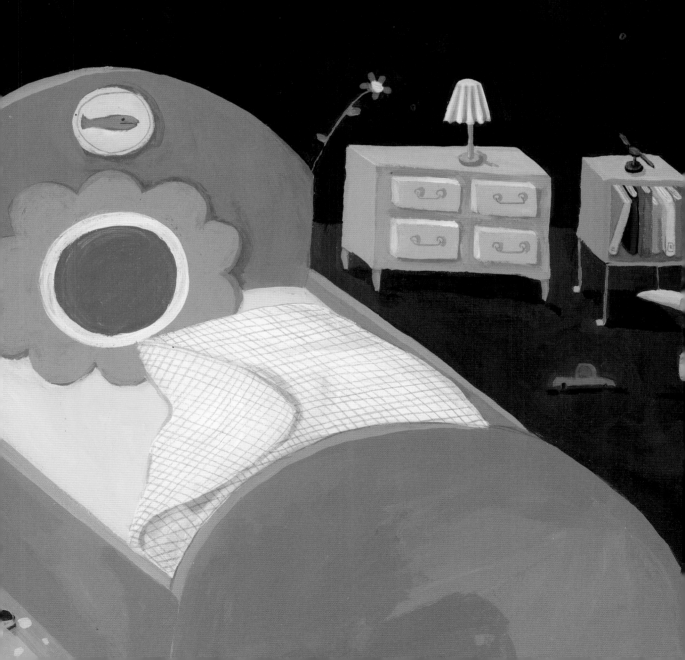

Are you a stork? No. That's why that doesn't work either. Every creature sleeps differently.

Fish sleep with their eyes open. They can't close them at all because they don't have eyelids. To sleep, they often hide in caves or cracks in the rocks. Pufferfish like to float on their backs while sleeping.

Mama, I can't sleep.

I tried the fish trick and kept my eyes open.
But they keep closing again.
And the bathtub is hard and uncomfortable.

You're not a fish either.
Every creature sleeps differently.
Bats sleep with their heads down.

They hang by their feet from a branch or a beam in the attic. That way they're safe from enemies. If there's any danger, they let go and fly away, as quick as a flash.

Mama, I can't sleep.
Even though I wanted to do it like a bat.
Now my head is really heavy.
And the hanging bar is digging into the backs of my knees.
I can perform in the circus like this, but not sleep.

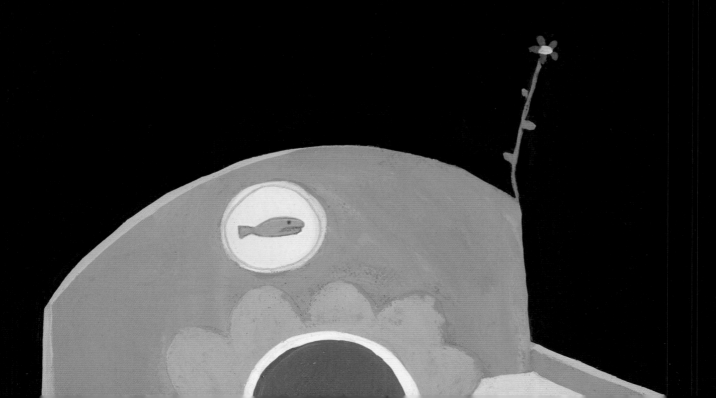

Are you a bat or a child?
Every creature sleeps
differently.

Ducks sleep in a group.
The ducks sitting on the outside quickly open one eye over
and over again while they're sleeping.
They keep watch to see if a fox or other enemy is coming.

Mama, I can't sleep

Neither can my dolls
It's so hard to open and close on
eye quickly while you're sleeping
And to do it over and over
I'll never be able to do tha
all night long. Thank goodness n
foxes will come into our house

You're not a duck either. That's why it doesn't work.
Every creature sleeps differently.

Dogs love to sleep in cozy beds. They turn around in a circle before sleeping and make a nice comfortable spot. Then they curl up on it.

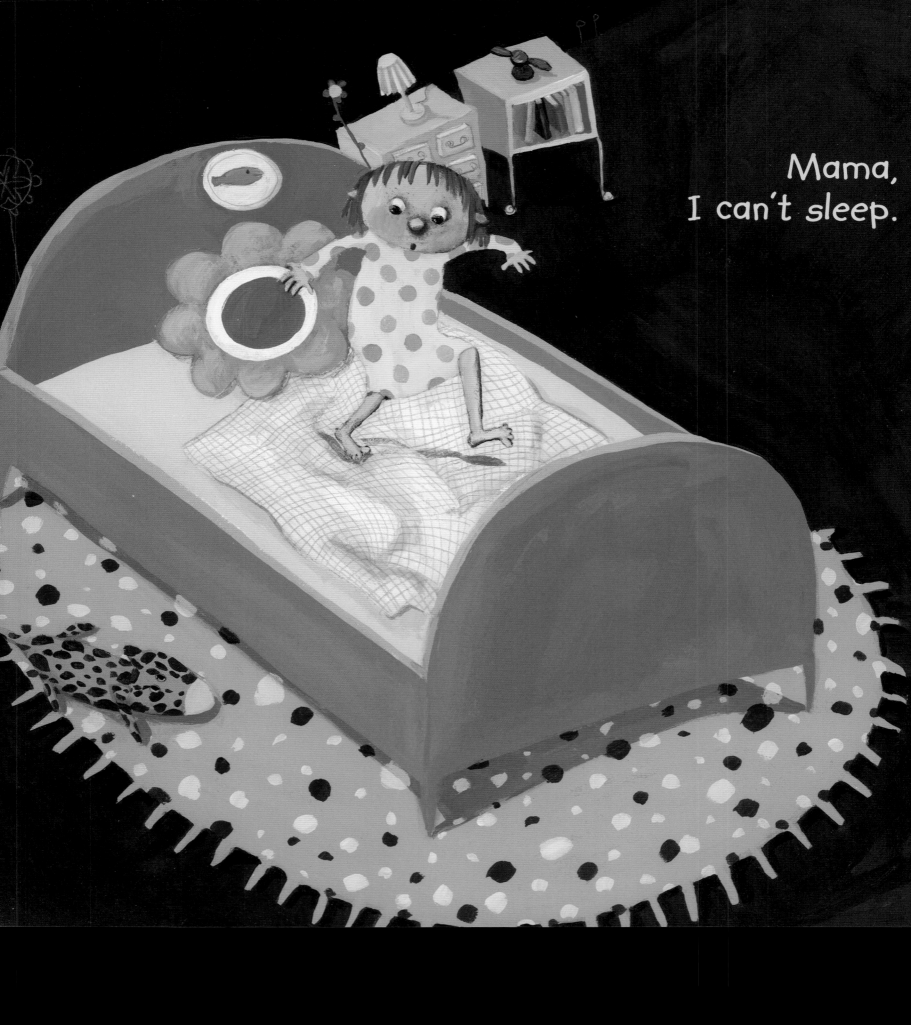

Mama,
I can't sleep.

I'm completely awake from trampling around. I don't understand how a dog is tired after that and can fall asleep.

hat only works for dogs and not for children.
Every creature sleeps differently.
But now it's late, and you really have to sleep.
Because while you're sleeping, you grow.
And when you're big, you can go to bed later.
Really big animals, like giraffes, sleep very little, by the way.
Four hours is enough for them.

Good night, Mama.
I'm sleeping now.
Then soon I'll be as big as a giraffe.

Visit our website at www.skyponypress.com.

10 9 8 7 6 5 4 3 2 1

Manufactured in China, August 2014
This product conforms to CPSIA 2008

Library of Congress Cataloging-in-Publication Data

ISBN: 978-1-63450-061-6